Dear Bob,
  I hope you enjoy
the book!
  I love you!
  aunt Cathy

# The Sailing Challenge

BEAR GRYLLS ADVENTURES

## The BEAR GRYLLS ADVENTURES series

# The Sailing Challenge

## Bear Grylls

### Illustrated by Emma McCann

Bear
Grylls

First American Edition 2021
Kane Miller, A Division of EDC Publishing

First published in Great Britain in 2019 by Bear Grylls, an imprint
of Bonnier Zaffre, a Bonnier Publishing Company
Text and illustrations copyright © Bear Grylls Ventures, 2019
Illustrations by Emma McCann

For information contact:
Kane Miller, A Division of EDC Publishing
PO Box 470663
Tulsa, OK 74147-0663
**www.kanemiller.com**
**www.usbornebooksandmore.com**

Library of Congress Control Number: 2020941012

Printed and bound in the United States of America
1 2 3 4 5 6 7 8 9 10

ISBN: 978-1-68464-237-3

*To the young survivor*
*reading this book for the first time.*
*May your eyes always be wide open*
*to adventure, and your heart full*
*of courage and determination to*
*see your dreams through.*

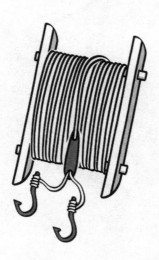

1

# FIVE TO TWO

Left or right, left or right …

Mia had reached a fork in the path. Left was the way to the camp office. Right was the tents. Mia had to get her swimming gear from her tent, but she also needed to get to the office before two o'clock. She hesitated.

"Hey, Mia, we haven't got long! Are you coming?" Her friend Lily was heading toward the office.

Mia immediately set off down the path on the right to the tents. "I need to get my gear. I'll catch you later, Lily."

"But we've got to sign up on the board by two o'clock for tomorrow's activities! And that's …" Lily checked her watch, "in five minutes!"

They had already had this argument at lunchtime, and Mia knew what Lily was going to say. But instead of waiting, she called out, "It'll be fine," and started walking toward the tents. She hoped Lily would get the hint. Mia hated being hassled to do things. She preferred to do things in her own time, in her own way.

"But if you don't sign up for what you want," Lily went on, "they just put you down for any old thing where there's a space."

2

Mia knew Lily was right. But somehow she just couldn't change her mind now.

"So?" Mia gave a big, couldn't-careless shrug. "That's cool. Maybe I'll get something fun."

"Yes, or maybe you'll get wildflower spotting, and you'll nearly die of hay fever again!"

Mia laughed it off.

"Hey, they won't put me down for that again, not after last time."

"I know." Lily tried to sound patient. "They might put you down for something even *worse*, Mia! Why don't you just tell me what you want to sign up for, then I can put your name down on the sheet?"

"Look, it'll be fine," Mia called over her shoulder, as she headed for the tents. "I'll sort it out later. But you'd better hurry up or you'll miss the sign-up yourself!"

Lily hopped from one foot to the other in frustration, but then she turned and hurried off toward the bulletin board.

The moment she was gone, all Mia's confidence vanished. She knew Lily had been right, really. She just couldn't bear to admit it. She scuffed her feet and sulked silently as she headed for the tents.

It had been like this for as long as Mia could remember. Whenever someone tried to make a rule or suggest she should do something, she always wanted to do something different. Mia had been all set to make the two o'clock deadline for today – until Lily had reminded her at lunch. Right away it was like every part of Mia's body decided that it didn't want to sign up. Not even if it meant risking being put in an activity she didn't enjoy.

Mia was confused and angry and upset with herself. She was going to get something really terrible tomorrow, now, wasn't she? Maybe not wildflowers.

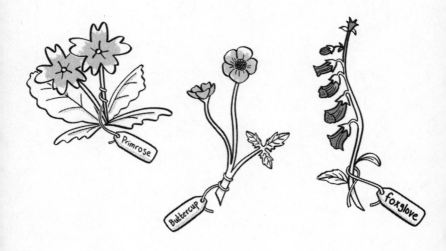

The camp staff had probably gotten the message about that. But something else boring, probably.

Mia gave herself a shake. Maybe she had blown her chances for tomorrow, but there was still tube polo today, and she enjoyed that. She grabbed her swimming gear and a spare T-shirt from the tent, and hurried off.

## 2

# NO CARRYING!

The umpire was blowing her whistle outside by the pool while Mia was still in the locker room. She quickly stuffed all her things into her locker. Something dropped out and narrowly missed her bare toes.

"Whoa!"

It was that compass Joe had given to her. She hoped it hadn't been damaged by hitting the tile floor. Its needle was going around and around and somehow it seemed to have five directions on it. Mia didn't have time to study it. She put it back in the locker, strapped the key to her wrist and hurried out.

Mia was the last to arrive at the outdoor pool. Eleven other boys and girls were all there in their swimming gear and T-shirts. Inner tubes bobbed in the water.

"Now, let's give you all a quick check." The leader walked among them. "Everyone got a T-shirt?" she said. "Unprotected backs and shoulders might get sunburned. Tommy, no goggles, I'm afraid. I know the chlorine stings, but you could injure your eyes if someone knocked you. Mia, that looks like a new T-shirt. Do you really want to wear it? The chlorine will bleach it."

Mia hadn't thought of that. She had just grabbed the nearest T-shirt she had. It was a new one, a birthday present, only worn a couple of times.

"It's fine, thanks," Mia told her. Inside, she was upset not to have realized that herself. But now that the leader had pointed it out she didn't want to take the suggestion. Instead she quietly said goodbye to the shirt's cheerful patterns and colors.

The leader raised her eyebrows, but didn't say any more about it. She went on to remind everyone of the rules, and put them into teams with yellow and red armbands. Mia was on the Yellow team.

Tube polo was designed so that you didn't have to be a strong swimmer. Players sat in inflated inner tubes, and pushed themselves around the pool with their hands. The teams took up their positions. The umpire blew her whistle and chucked the ball into the middle of the pool.

Both teams splashed toward it, eager paddling hands sending up clouds of spray. Mia was at the back of the Yellow team. A boy on her team got to the ball first. He quickly passed it, but a girl on the Red team caught it and chucked it to another boy on the far side of the pool.

Half the Yellows started to paddle-charge toward him – but not Mia. Mia had worked out that the Reds would have to pass it again, so she might as well stay put and wait.

Sure enough, the ball suddenly flew out of the mass of laughing, splashing kids toward her. Mia grabbed it with both hands. She dropped it onto her lap, and started to paddle as hard as she could toward the far end.

The whistle blew.

"Mia! That counts as carrying."

The Reds cheered, and Mia's jaw dropped.

"I'm not carrying! I'm not using my hands!"

"Mia, you can only touch or move the ball with one hand, unless you're the goalie. I did say! Free throw to the Reds."

"Oh, that is so unfair ..." Mia muttered.

But the Reds got their throw, and it

soon led to the first goal of the game. Mia felt like she was getting dirty looks from the other Yellows.

"How should I know it counted as carrying?" she moaned. But no one was listening.

Mia spent the next couple of minutes in a sulk. The ball flew back and forth between the teams and the sides of the pool.

Then suddenly it splashed down in front of her.

Mia scooped it up with one hand and looked around for a Yellow to pass it to. But she was surrounded by Reds, all paddle-charging toward her like a fleet of battleships.

Suddenly Mia felt herself sinking. Her tube was leaking. She could hear the hiss

and see the bubbles as air squirted out of the valve. In a moment she was up to her waist in water.

"Sinking!" she shouted. "Not fair …"

All the Reds arrived at the same time. Someone snatched the ball away. Mia kicked herself away from her deflated tube, but the other tubes all around her made it impossible to see anything.

In a moment the umpire would have to blow her whistle for a time-out. The game couldn't go on if one of the players was out of action.

Mia got out of the crowd the only way she could – by swimming down, kicking and struggling in a mass of bubbles and legs. She opened her eyes underwater and they immediately started stinging. The light was strangely blue. She turned and kicked her way to the surface and gasped for air. Water sluiced over her head and she palmed it away from her eyes. Some of it dripped into her open mouth.

Yuck! It was salty.

Mia blinked her eyes open against the stinging.

She was submerged up to her neck, treading water.

But she wasn't in the swimming pool.

"What?"

Hot sun beat down on her. There was nothing but blue, choppy water under a cloudless sky, all the way to the horizon.

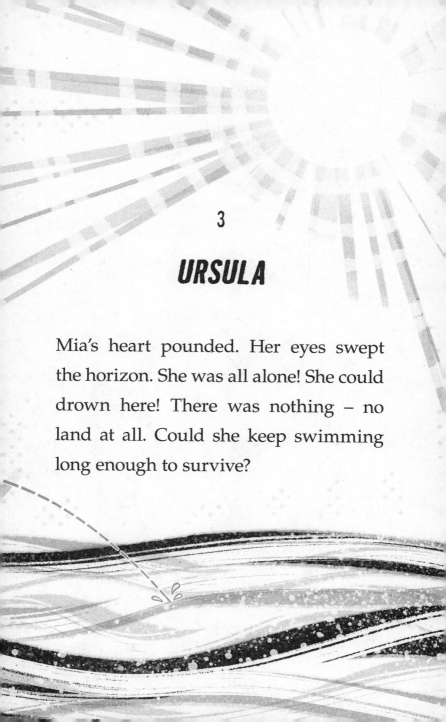

## 3

# URSULA

Mia's heart pounded. Her eyes swept the horizon. She was all alone! She could drown here! There was nothing – no land at all. Could she keep swimming long enough to survive?

Then she saw the boat.

It was wooden, about as long as a bus, with one mast and a pair of patched red sails. It was heading away from her and Mia could make out a man at the back end, standing over a spoked steering wheel. The name *Ursula* was painted on the back.

"Hey!" Mia shouted. "*Help*! Over here! Help!"

The man's head whipped around. He grabbed a U-shaped life buoy from the boat's rail and threw it toward Mia with all his strength. Even before it splashed into the water, he was spinning on the wheel and pulling on ropes. The boat began to turn.

Mia swam toward the life buoy. Its U-shape meant she could just pull it around her and float in the water. The boat was coming toward her. The man fiddled with more ropes and the sails collapsed down. The boat coasted to a stop.

Mia swam the last few strokes toward it, and the man leaned over the rail to help her up.

"Welcome on board *Ursula*!" he said, smiling. "How are you?"

Mia stood barefoot on the sun-warmed wooden deck while a small puddle of dripping water gathered around her.

"I'm okay, thank you!" she gasped. "But I don't know how long I could have kept going."

"You're a strong swimmer, but it's tough out there." The man was tall and tanned, in light, loose clothing and a fleece pullover. He had a hat with a brim that shaded his face as he smiled. "Between the sun, thirst, and the sharks, something would have gotten you sooner or later."

Mia looked at the sea and shuddered. She was glad to be standing on something solid, where sharks couldn't get.

"Um – where are we, exactly?" Mia asked. She looked around, but there was still absolutely no sign of anyone. Just a thousand miles of empty ocean in every direction. "It looks like the middle of nowhere."

The man laughed.

"I'd say that's exactly where we are. But I'm going to be your guide out of here." He held out his hand. "I'm Bear. Are you ready for some real adventure?"

Mia shook, cautiously.

"I'm Mia. Uh, what do you mean, *real* adventure?"

"Real, as in, a couple of hundred miles in a badly damaged boat?"

Mia quickly looked around.

"We're sinking?"

"Not quite, but *Ursula* got a bit beaten up by a storm a couple of days ago."

Now that Mia looked closer, she thought she could see the storm damage. She had already noticed the patched sails. The woodwork was all stained, like it had been soaked through and hadn't completely dried out yet.

"A lot of our supplies got swept away," Bear went on, "plus the dinghy, the radio antenna and self-steering gear. Some water got into the fuel so the engine's useless. The one thing we can still do is float, which fortunately doesn't take any effort on our part. We're heading for an island a couple of days away, where I'll make repairs."

"Are you sure the boat will make it?" Mia asked.

"Oh yes. We'll make it together," the man promised, with a smile. "The great thing about being at sea is that as long as you can stay alive, you know you'll make land eventually. The record for that's held by a guy called José Salvador Alvarenga, who managed to drift for thirteen months before hitting land. We'll be quicker than that, I promise."

Mia shivered suddenly. Despite the sun beating down, the sea breeze cut right through her in her wet swimsuit.

"Mia, you'd better get out of those wet things," Bear said quickly. "You'll find spare clothes in the locker down below, at the front of the cabin. Get something like mine, light enough to be cool but covering as much bare skin as you can. Sunburn can get you in a couple of hours."

"Thanks."

Mia made her way down a wooden ladder into the cabin. It was snug and cozy, with a bunk on each side and a little kitchen in one corner. But it smelled damp and she could see more damage wherever she looked. The walls were lined with wooden locker doors, and some were splintered and broken. A couple of windows had cracked. Everything looked like it had been thrown around.

She picked out some gear like Bear had described.

Suddenly the boat began to tilt slowly over to one side. Mia yelped in alarm and staggered to the ladder. If this boat was going to tip over, she didn't want to be trapped in the cabin.

"It's okay," Bear called from above. "We're just getting underway again."

Sure enough, *Ursula* found an angle to lean over at, and stuck to it. Mia quickly got dressed. She felt a lot better wrapped in warm, dry gear. She hadn't realized how much she was cooling down, even standing in the sunshine up on deck. She picked her way back across the leaning-over cabin, and took hold of the ladder to climb back onto deck.

Suddenly the whole boat shook and shuddered, as if it had run into a rock.

*But there are no rocks in the ocean*, Mia thought indignantly.

Another, harder shock ran through the boat. This time she heard the sound of splintering wood and running water. The blow knocked Mia to her knees. That was impossible! The boat had been lifted up!

"Hey, Mia!" Bear called urgently. "Get up here, quick!"

Mia quickly clambered onto deck. Bear's expression was taut and concentrating as he gripped the wheel. He nodded his head at the sea. Mia followed his gaze, and gasped.

All around them, huge, gray shapes, two or three times as big as *Ursula*, were breaking out of the sea. Mia recognized them from television and videos, but she had never known they were so *huge* in real life. One of them must have hit the boat just now.

"Whales!" she gasped.

# 4

# WHALE OF A TIME

"Are they attacking us?" Mia asked nervously. She had no idea what she and Bear could do if one of those mighty shapes took a real dislike to *Ursula*. But they didn't look aggressive.

"I think one of them just came up beneath us without looking up." Bear gripped the wheel and scanned the sea

ahead. "When you weigh over sixty-five thousand pounds you're probably going to be okay whatever you bump into, and a thirty-ton wooden boat is always going to come off worse."

Mia remembered the water sound in the cabin.

"Um, Bear," she gasped nervously. "It might have knocked a hole in us."

Bear made a face.

"*Ursula* is handling differently. I'll check properly once our friends are out of the way. Meanwhile, we both need to keep a sharp lookout. If it looks like another one of them is heading for us, point and yell."

"Point and yell," Mia agreed. "Right." That was one instruction that Mia was happy to follow.

Her gaze leapt from whale to whale. The whole herd was just cruising peacefully past. All she could see was their backs – ugly and bumpy and covered with tiny little shellfish. But they were still beautiful, and it was impossible to be angry with them. The whale hadn't attacked *Ursula*. It just hadn't noticed that there was anything there.

One of the whales blew out, with a sound like a steam engine letting off pressure. A cloud of white mist drifted over the boat. It stank of fish and the worst bad breath ever.

*"Whew!"* Mia waved her hand in front of her face. Okay, they were beautiful but they were definitely outstaying their welcome.

Suddenly a huge tail shaped like a giant letter Y began to rise out of the water, dead ahead. Water cascaded off its two halves, which were the size of aircraft wings.

There was a whale right in front of them. Bear spun the wheel to turn. The tail rose up, and up, and up. The whale must have been standing on its nose. Then it began to slide down into the sea. The tail slapped down with a mighty crash, and water sluiced over the front deck. The whole boat rocked, from end to end and side to side.

*Ursula* had turned away from the whale in front – but now Mia saw another danger. A massive gray bumpy

back was surfacing like a submarine just a few yards away.

"Whale coming up behind!" she shouted. Bear started to turn the wheel again, but too late. The enormous back slid closer and closer, and then there was a crunch and *Ursula* shook again. The boat spun around in the water, with its two humans clinging on for dear life.

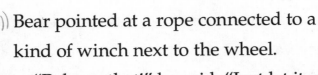

Bear pointed at a rope connected to a kind of winch next to the wheel.

"Release that!" he said. "Just let it go."

Mia fumbled with the rope, while Bear did the same to a similar rope on the other side of the wheel. Mia's rope suddenly came loose and whizzed through her fingers. At the same time the sail at the front dropped down to the deck. The main sail dropped down a moment later as Bear released his rope. The loose canvas waggled around in the wind.

Bear passed Mia a handful of bungee cords.

"See if you can tie the main sail to the boom, and the

foresail to the rail, to stop them flapping. I need to inspect the damage."

It wasn't easy, but Mia worked out how to do what Bear had asked. She could bunch up a bundle of sail canvas in her arms, and press it to the boom, and then wrap the bungee cord around it. She did the same with the front sail – what Bear called the foresail – tying it to *Ursula*'s rail.

The whales had all passed by and Mia and Bear were alone in the sea again. Suddenly a hatch in the deck at Mia's feet flew open.

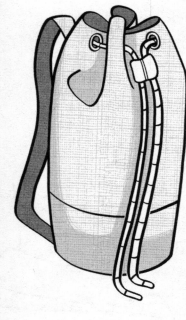

Bear was down below, pushing up a large canvas bag with both hands.

"Can you take this, please?"

Mia helped drag the heavy bag up onto deck. Bear clambered up after it.

"That first knock split some planks just behind the bow," he said. "Water's coming in below."

Mia stared.

"You mean – we're sinking?"

"Only very slowly. Let's make it even slower."

Bear opened the bag and tipped its contents out onto the deck. Mia realized it was another sail, all folded up tight. Bear unfurled it to its full length, and then with Mia's help he folded it double, then double again, until it was its full length, but only a quarter of its width.

"Now," Bear said, "we're going to pass this under the boat, and fasten it in place."

They each took one end of the folded sail and lowered it into the sea on either side of *Ursula*'s pointy front end. They let it sink down and then they slowly walked backward on opposite sides of the deck, taking their ends of the sail with them.

"This is the place," Bear said when they were about three yards back from the front end. "Now, hold on to both ends. You'll have to grip tight."

Mia held on to her end with one hand, and reached across to take Bear's end of the folded sail with the other. The sail tugged and jerked. It was heavy and hard to get a grip on. Her fingers ached and she just wanted to let go.

And she almost did, before she remembered one thing that was kind of important. This sail was meant to stop *Ursula* from sinking.

So Mia held on.

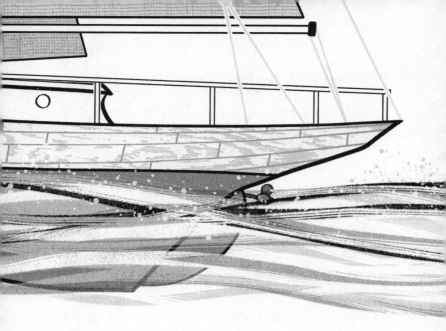

Bear whipped a length of rope through metal eyelets set into the ends of the sail, tying the two ends together. At last Mia could let go. She worked out that the sail was now wrapped completely around the hull, pressed tight against the damaged planks and held in place by the rope. Bear dropped down through the hatch for a moment, and emerged again looking pleased.

"That did the trick, just like it did two hundred years ago for Admiral Nelson. He had to patch up cannonball damage, but the idea's the same."

"Is it waterproof?" Mia asked.

Bear smiled.

"No, but water pressure is pushing it against the hull to seal the hole – the water will still come through, slowly. We're going to have to pump, regularly and often."

Mia felt mostly relieved. Bear sounded more relaxed so she guessed that much of the danger was over. They weren't going to sink. She didn't really listen to Bear's comment about pumping.

Bear puffed his cheeks out.

"We'd better have some water and some rations before we do the next part. That last knock caused even more damage."

Mia's brief feeling of being okay suddenly vanished.

"Another hole?" she asked in alarm. Bear had already said that *Ursula*'s dinghy was swept away in the storm. If the boat went down now, then there was nowhere for them to go.

"Fortunately, no. But it took away the rudder. We've got no way to steer. Right now, we're just drifting out of control."

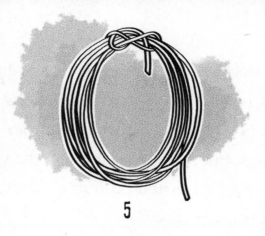

5

# MIXED MESSAGES

"Eighty-five ..." Mia gasped. "Eighty-six ..."

Sweat poured down her face as she heaved on the pump handle. Her arm was killing her. On the other side of the hull, water gushed out of the boat and into the sea with every stroke.

The handle was tucked away behind the ladder. When Mia had first gone down below, water had been sloshing on the floorboards. Up on deck, she'd only half listened to Bear's instructions. She had been too busy thinking of her own things. But as soon as she saw the water she quickly started pumping. Obviously this was serious.

Every heave felt like she was moving a ton of water.

"Eighty-seven ... eighty-eight ..."

Bear was on deck, doing more repairs. Bear had suggested that Mia count to a hundred strokes, to make the time pass more easily. Then start again with another hundred, and keep repeating until *Ursula* was dry.

Mia had lost count of how many times she had gotten up to eighty-eight, and kept going. Her arm was aching with the unusual effort.

Surely a quick break couldn't hurt?

Mia paused, and flexed her throbbing arm with relief. But as soon as the pump was quiet, she could hear the water sloshing below.

There was no easy way out of this, she realized. Just pumping.

Mia gritted her teeth and started again.

"Eighty-nine …"

On top of all that, there was a really weird smell in the cabin, which made her gag. It was like something had died beneath the boards. Bear said it was the bilges. There was always somewhere, right at the lowest part of the boat, where the pump couldn't reach. The water down there was stagnant and foul. The flood of seawater had mixed with the bilge water and brought it all up close to the cabin. Every slosh sent a signal to her stomach that she wanted to be sick. She fought it back.

"Ninety … ninety-one … "

The pump made a gurgling, sucking sound, and suddenly moved more easily. There was almost no resistance.

Mia had done it! She had pumped the water out of the boat!

She scrambled back up onto the deck and gratefully breathed the fresh air. The rotten bilge smell still seemed to be lodged inside her, at the back of her throat.

"We're dry, Bear!" she gasped. "For now." She knew that more water would already be leaking in through the sail patch.

Bear looked up from what he had been working on, and grinned.

"Terrific!" he beamed. "Great work, Mia. If we give it a hundred strokes every hour from now on, that should do it. Now, could you get me a length of rope from the second locker along?"

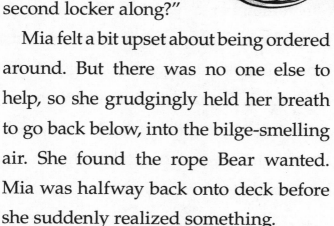

Mia felt a bit upset about being ordered around. But there was no one else to help, so she grudgingly held her breath to go back below, into the bilge-smelling air. She found the rope Bear wanted. Mia was halfway back onto deck before she suddenly realized something.

Bear had told her where the rope was,

and she had been able to go straight there, instead of fussing around in the stinking air, trying to find it. *Ursula* had a place for everything, and everything was in its place.

It must have taken time and effort to get the boat like that, but it was obviously worth it. Mia knew that the word "shipshape" means being tidy and well ordered. She could see why. She remembered what her bedroom at home looked like, and how her parents were always nagging her to get more organized. She usually ignored them.

She climbed quickly back onto deck before she passed out from the smell, and handed the rope over.

Bear had taken a washboard – a flat piece of wood that had been slotted into the cabin entrance to keep the weather out. It had ventilation slots cut into it and he had fastened it to one end of an oar, looping the rope through the slots.

At the other end of the oar he had tied on a wooden pin, sticking out at right angles, with a kind of X-shaped knot that lashed around it, over and over again – top left to bottom right, bottom left to top right. It all looked pretty complicated to Mia, but she guessed what it was for.

"Is that our new rudder?"

Bear nodded.

"Sure is. Do you think you can help me fix it in place?"

Together they lowered the oar into the sea by the back rail, next to one of the vertical rail supports. Mia held it in place while Bear lashed it to the rail with the rope she had brought him, using another of those X-knots. Then he tied another around the oar and the bottom of the rail support, so that the oar was held in two places.

"That will stop it from flopping around," Bear said. He gave the wooden pin an experimental push. The oar turned left and right in its knot supports, but it stayed attached to the rail.

"Okay. Once we're moving again, this should give us a bit of control ..."

Suddenly Mia felt her guts give a heave inside her. She clutched her middle and gulped. A moment later it was like her entire stomach wanted to crawl up out of her mouth. She leaned quickly over the back end of the boat and vomited into the sea.

"It's seasickness," Bear said with sympathy. "The motion sensor in your inner ear tells you that you're moving, but the cabin seems to be staying still, so your brain gets mixed messages and the result is that you feel sick. A strong smell like the bilge water can just make it worse. Hold on."

Bear was back a moment later, with a piece of cloth, and a couple of mugs of water. He tore the cloth into two strips.

"There's an acupressure technique ..." he said as he wadded one strip up into a tight little ball. "You press on your wrist, and that stimulates the nerve, which is more specific than the mixed messages the brain is getting, so it helps the brain

ignore them. So press this against your wrist …"

Mia held the wadded cloth against her skin with a finger, while Bear wrapped the other strip tight around it, tying it off in a knot to hold it firm. The wad pressed into the skin of her wrist.

"You can't walk around pressing your wrist all the time, so this has the same effect. You can also try looking at the horizon. It looks like it's moving, even though it isn't, so your brain gets the same message from eyes and ears."

Mia usually hated it when people gave her "good advice." Especially grown-ups. But looking at the horizon really did seem to help. Besides, she really didn't want to throw up again.

"How are you feeling?" Bear asked after a little while.

"Less sick now," Mia agreed. "Thanks."

Bear smiled, and passed her a pill from a bottle.

"This is for rehydration. Vomiting makes your body lose water and salt, and neither of us can afford that."

Mia popped it into her mouth, and reached gratefully for one of the mugs. The vomit had left a taste in her mouth and she wanted it gone. Bear took the other mug. They both drank at the same time – and immediately spat it out.

"It's salty!" Mia exclaimed. The water was disgusting.

"Yup," Bear said gravely. "That's not good. If the sea has gotten into our water tank that means we can't use it. Not a drop."

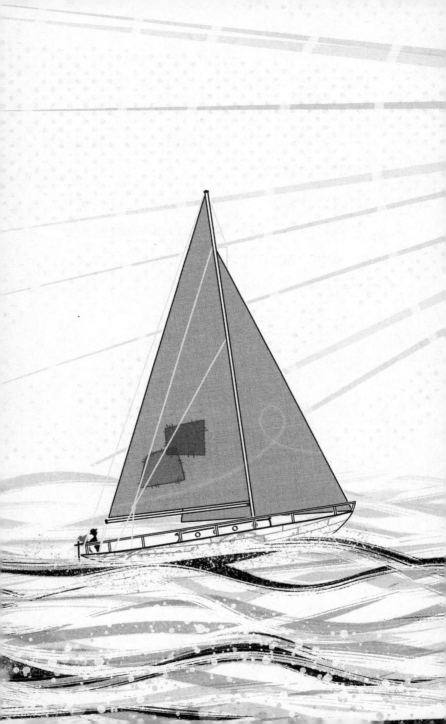

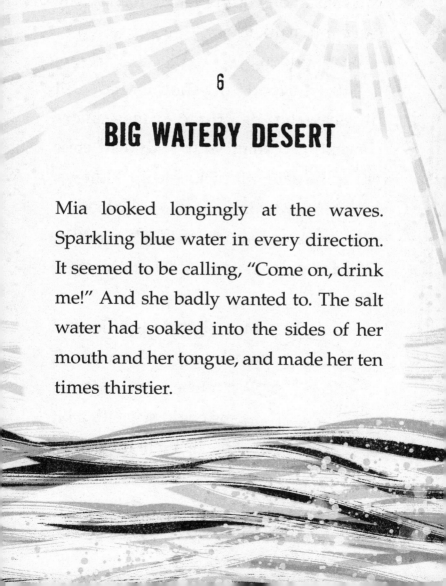

# 6

# BIG WATERY DESERT

Mia looked longingly at the waves. Sparkling blue water in every direction. It seemed to be calling, "Come on, drink me!" And she badly wanted to. The salt water had soaked into the sides of her mouth and her tongue, and made her ten times thirstier.

"I know you're not supposed to drink salt water," she said, "but why not? You can eat salt on your potato chips, so why can't you drink it too?"

Bear nodded.

"It's a good question, Mia. Salt in seawater is three times more concentrated than your body can cope with," he said. "It pickles your kidneys, which filter toxins out of your blood. If you drink too much, it'll kill you. So, the basic rule is – do *not* drink seawater. Ever."

Mia sighed and looked back at the ocean. It stretched out as far as she could see. "It's a bit like being in the desert,

isn't it? We're surrounded by this stuff that's dangerous to us."

"One big, watery desert," Bear agreed with a smile. "But there are ways to cope. Right now our number one priority is to get moving again."

Together they hauled the sails back up and Bear got them back on course, cautiously handling their new tiller.

"It works," he decided, "but it's very sensitive. It'll need constant attention. Mia, I'm going to have to leave some things up to you. I'd better brief you."

"So, you're going to tell me what to do," Mia said without thinking, and her brain shut down. It was automatic. An adult was giving instructions, so they went in one ear

61

and straight out the other.

But today Mia overrode her brain. She forced herself to start listening. This was life-and-death stuff out here. It was important. Bear was talking about water.

"... I estimate the island will be no more than three days away, and we each need at least one liter of water per day. So that's a total of two liters per day for three days ..."

"Six liters," Mia calculated.

"There's bottled water in the locker under the sink. See how much we have, and bring one of the bottles up."

Mia popped quickly back into the cabin, holding her breath. She counted the bottles, and her heart sank. She took one back on deck.

"We've got four liters, including this

one," she reported reluctantly. Bear opened the bottle thoughtfully.

"So, we need to ration ourselves, and supplement what we have."

He took a mouthful from the bottle, but didn't swallow it immediately. He gargled it, then swilled it around in his mouth, then licked his lips, then swallowed. He handed Mia the bottle.

"Take a mouthful."

Mia was so thirsty that she gulped it down before Bear had finished.

"Whoa! Hang on there … do what I just did and swill it around your mouth first. It helps the water soak in so you get as much good as you can from it."

Mia took more care with the next

mouthful. The water moistened her mouth and made her less thirsty than she had been.

"Now," Bear said, "I need you to get more stuff out of the cabin. There's a big bowl and a pair of metal cups in the locker by the stove. There's a plastic sheet under the bunk and a couple of fishing weights and bungee cords from the locker up here … Can you get all that for me, please?"

Mia could feel herself wanting to tell Bear to get it himself, but she resisted. She knew that they were in a bit of trouble and that he needed her to do what he said. She decided to trust him. Besides, being busy helped take Mia's mind off feeling ill. She quickly followed Bear's instructions.

"That's great," he said as she added the last item to the pile on the deck. "Thanks, Mia. Now can you set the bowl down on the cabin roof? It needs to be as flat as possible."

The cabin roof was pointed, but because *Ursula* leaned over while they were under sail, one side of the roof was almost flat.

"Okay, now put one of the cups in the middle of the bowl. Weigh it down with one of the fishing weights. Scoop up some seawater with the other cup and fill the bowl until it's about an inch deep."

Mia did all that, but she left out the weight for the cup. What was the point of that? She poured the seawater into the pan, and the cup started to float. Now Mia saw the point of the weight. She

quickly rescued the cup before it toppled over into the salt water, and dropped the weight in.

"Now put the plastic sheet over the bowl loosely, so that it dips down in the middle. Use another weight to make sure it stays dipped, directly over the cup inside. Fix the sheet in place with a bungee cord around the rim …"

Eventually Mia had it set up like Bear said.

"What does this do?" she asked.

"It's called a solar still. The sun will warm up the seawater, so it will start to evaporate and leave the salt behind. It will condense on the plastic and turn back into liquid …"

"And trickle into the cup!" Mia realized happily.

"That's right! It won't get us much –
maybe half a liter a day at most. But it
should help us close the gap. That will
get us five and a half liters out of the total
six that we need. We'll leave a tarpaulin
out at night to collect any dew on deck –
that's another source of fresh water ..."

Suddenly Mia barely heard Bear. There
had been a flash of light from behind him.
The sun reflecting off glass or metal. She
ran to the back rail and stared.

"What is it, Mia?"

"There's a ship behind us! Look!" She
pointed to a tiny blob on the horizon.

Bear grabbed some binoculars. "Great
spot, Mia! It's an oil tanker. Fetch a flare
from the locker, there. One with an
orange top."

The locker was full of metal tubes like

batons. Mia grabbed the
nearest one and
passed it to Bear,
but he shook his
head.

"I don't
really want
to let go of
the tiller. You do it.
Point it away from
you, aim it up into
the sky, and give that cord on the end a
hard yank ..."

Mia did, and she almost dropped the
tube in surprise. It went off with a bang.
An orange ball of fire shot into the air
and floated down again like a mini sun.

"Shouldn't we turn around toward
it?" she asked.

"We'd better not. The water flow could rip the patch sail away, and if they don't see us then we're just wasting time going back the way we came. We won't catch up to them. They've got engines, they can come to us – *if* they see us ..."

Mia and Bear eagerly fixed their eyes on the shape on the horizon, waiting for it to turn toward them.

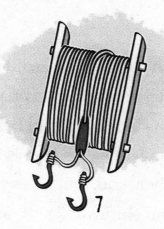

7

# POSITIVE ATTITUDE

Mia quickly realized two things.

One was that she was holding her breath, and starting to feel a little dizzy. She started to breathe normally again.

The other was that the oil tanker was sailing on without changing course. Slowly the dark blob disappeared below the horizon, and that was that. Mia felt the disappointment hanging on her shoulders like weights.

"They didn't see us," she said sadly.

"I'm afraid it's something you get used to in situations like this," said Bear. "And I'll tell you someone else who isn't going to see us either, and they're even closer to us than that ship was."

Mia looked around. There were no other ships. Was Bear talking about a submarine?

"Who? Where?"

Bear smiled and pointed straight up. Mia craned her head back. A thin white line was slowly drawing itself across the blue sky.

"An airplane?" Mia said.

Bear nodded again.

"It's five miles up, so it's closer than that ship on the horizon was. You'll see several planes during the day, and you

can bet not one of them will see us. It can feel like they're ignoring you deliberately, but you can't let it get you down. Depression is a killer for a survivor, so …" Bear tapped his head. "You don't let it in. Think of the *good* things we have. A boat. A destination. The ability to get there. There have been people worse off than us, and they managed, so we can too."

"Who had it worse?" Mia asked out of curiosity.

"Well, in 1789, a British navy captain called William Bligh managed to sail four thousand miles with eighteen men, in an open twenty-three-foot boat – smaller than *Ursula* and with no cabin. He only lost one man in forty-seven days."

"That's pretty good," Mia agreed.

"Of course, he was a terrible captain." Bear smiled. "That's why he was in that boat in the first place. His men had thrown him off his ship. But he was an amazing sailor and navigator. One thing he knew all about was keeping his men's spirits up. They had to be kept busy. And so do we. So, how about we try to catch some food?"

Mia was alarmed. First the water, now food?

"You mean we don't have anything to eat on board?"

"Well, we do have cans, but there's nothing like the buzz of catching your own fresh food. There's some fishing twine and hooks in the locker by the wheel there ..."

Mia found the reel of orange twine. One end had a hook with some bait dangling from it. The other was attached to the reel itself.

"Mind the hook," Bear cautioned. He was still holding on to the tiller, not able to move away from it. "You can easily cut yourself. Right, start to unwind the line into the sea. When you get to the end, tie it to the stern rail ..."

Mia let the hook down into the sea. It flashed and danced below the surface as *Ursula* pulled it along and the twine slowly stretched out behind them. After about fifteen feet, the line was at full stretch.

Bear had said to tie it to the stern rail, but Mia couldn't see the point in that. How would they know if they had caught something? Didn't fishermen feel the tug on their line when they had hooked a fish?

Bear wasn't watching. He was concentrating on steering. So Mia decided to wrap the end of the line around her finger instead. That way she would feel the tug straightaway.

A few moments later Mia realized why she should have tied the line to the rail. The drag of the line through the water pulled it tight. The twine felt like someone trying to bite off Mia's finger.

Within seconds, her fingertip was numb and white. Mia stifled a scream and pulled at the line with her other hand to release the pressure.

*Okay, so Bear had been right,* Mia thought. There was only one way to do this. She tied the reel end of the line around the rail, like Bear had suggested.

"How do you know when you've caught something?" Mia asked.

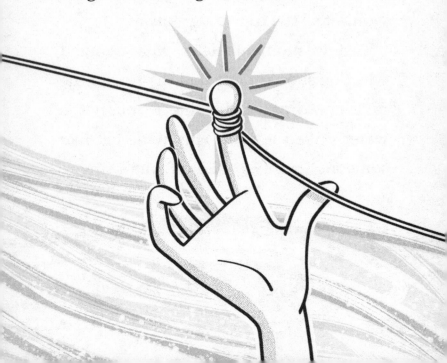

"Give the line a pull every now and then. If there's something there, you'll feel it. Now, how do you feel about taking the tiller for a while?"

"Me?" Mia gasped.

The biggest thing she had ever steered was her bike back home. *Ursula* was way bigger than that.

"I've been awake since before the storm," Bear pointed out. "However long you can keep going, there's always a point where it's better to take a rest. I don't want to get so tired that I end up making a mistake that could get us both killed. If you weren't here then I'd have to get the sails down and let *Ursula* drift while I had a nap. But I'd rather keep moving, and since you're here …"

Mia saw what he meant. But even so it

was scary.

"You will stay to check that I'm doing it right?" she asked nervously.

Bear smiled.

"Don't worry, I'll stay up here until I'm sure you've got it."

"Okay."

Bear moved over to one side, still keeping hold of the tiller. Mia cautiously took his place and wrapped her fingers around the wooden pin. Mia had control of *Ursula*.

8

# MIA IN CHARGE

The tiller trembled beneath Mia's hands. Every now and then it tried to give a strong jerk to the left or the right.

"It wants to go all over the place," she said.

"Well, sailing is one big balancing act between the sails and the keel and the rudder. We've lost our normal rudder and we're using a washboard attached to an oar, so we're unbalanced. So yes,

the boat wants to go all over the place, but we can't let it. Now, we want to steer a course of two hundred and ninety degrees."

There was a compass the size of a dinner plate in a glass case next to the wheel. The dial was marked with the four main directions, and every ten degrees in between. If it had been a clock face then 290 degrees would have been where ten o'clock was.

Mia tried to keep *Ursula* on course, but the compass swung back and forth.

"The waves keep knocking us all over," Mia protested.

Bear smiled.

"Don't try to exactly correct the

course every time we bounce one way or another. The best we can do is stick to the right course generally, as close as we can. Also, the person steering has to keep an eye on the wind."

He pointed.

"See those telltales, those pieces of cloth tied to the ropes, blowing in the wind? They show the direction the wind is coming from. You can see that at the moment it's coming from the front right, and we're sailing at an angle to it. That means we have the sails hauled in quite tight. If the wind shifts farther forward, we'll pull the sails in a bit more, and if it comes back, we'll let the sails out. So, the wind pushes on the sails one way, the water pushes against the keel the other way, and the boat moves like someone squeezing an orange seed between two fingers ..."

"It moves forward," Mia realized. Bear nodded.

"The wind's like the boat, always moving a little from side to side, and that's fine. If it changes big time, then you have to adjust the sails, using these winches."

There were winches on either side of *Ursula*, with ropes that led to the end of the foresail. A third rope was attached to the end of the boom. Bear showed how to either turn the handles on the winches to tighten the sails, or how to release the winches and let the sails out.

"Now, how's the line doing?"

Bear tugged on the line streaming behind *Ursula*.

"Hello! We have something!"

He pulled the line in, hand over hand. Something big and silver flashed and thrashed at the end of it. Their catch was putting up a fight. Mia felt she should go and help Bear, but she couldn't let go of the tiller.

"A Pacific cod!" Bear sounded pleased.

"About twenty pounds, I'd say. There's enough here to keep us going for a good while."

Bear got the thrashing fish into a bucket and then disappeared with it down below. Mia concentrated hard on keeping the tiller in the right place. Between watching the sails, the waves and the compass, it was hard work and took all her concentration.

Bear was soon back up on deck with a couple of bowls in his hands. One was full of pinky white flesh.

"That was quick," said Mia.

Bear laughed as he laid the strips of fresh fish out on the cabin roof, next to the solar still.

"The sun will dry these out, and we can eat them later. But this," he said, holding the second bowl toward her, "we'll use now."

He pulled out a fleshy lump the size of a plum. Bear squeezed it into a cup, and oily, yellow liquid slowly dripped out between his fingers.

"Now, this is a bit smelly, but cod liver oil makes an excellent sunscreen." Bear smiled at Mia. "I'm tough and weather beaten, but your skin is fairer than mine and I'd say you're starting to burn."

Mia winced.

"You're not rubbing that on me!" she exclaimed.

Bear grinned.

"You're right, Mia. I'm not. You are. Sunburn is a killer. It dehydrates you and it harms your skin, which is your body's first line of defense."

Mia had to admit that her face was starting to feel hot and dry, and there was no point suffering painfully if it could be avoided. So, she reluctantly dipped a finger into the fish oil and smeared it over her face and nose. She tried to ignore the fish smell.

"And now …" Bear stretched. "I really do need that break. Can I leave you in charge for an hour? I'll do the pumping, then rest."

Mia felt she had the hang of *Ursula*'s ways now. She gripped the tiller confidently.

"I'm pretty sure I can," she said.

"You're doing really well, Mia. Give me a shout if you need me."

Bear disappeared down below, and Mia was on her own.

*Yeah, I can do this*, she told herself.

*Ursula* was nudging off course again. Mia gently tweaked the tiller to get the compass back to 290 degrees.

The wind against her face seemed to shift slightly. Mia glanced at the cloth telltales. Sure enough, they were swinging around a bit.

Mia reached for the nearest winch. Then her hand paused. Did she really need to adjust the sails every time the wind bounced around a bit? Maybe she should save her energy.

The telltales showed that the wind

was still moving. Suddenly *Ursula* began to shake. The foresail went loose. The boom and the main sail swung over, with an enormous *crash* that shook the timbers.

Mia cringed and pulled on the winch. The boom swung back, more gently. The sails filled with wind and went taut again. *Ursula* ran smoothly again.

"Are you okay, Mia?" Bear called.

"Yes, fine!" Mia nodded frantically. "Yes, totally, absolutely, thanks."

Bear didn't say anything else. *Ursula* sailed on, with Mia a little wiser at the helm.

9

# LAND HO

Mia stirred sleepily in her bunk. It was still dark, but the alarm clock on the shelf by her head was beeping. Time to get up and take her next watch.

Mia and Bear had spent the rest of the day taking turns at the tiller, and pumping, and generally keeping *Ursula* afloat and on course. They snacked on dried fish washed down with rationed mouthfuls of water. They had worked out their routine well, but by the time Mia had to turn in, she had been dead on her feet.

She had slept like a log, and now she felt completely refreshed – and excited. She was looking forward to getting back to work.

The first task was pumping water out. Then she climbed the ladder back onto deck. Bear was at the tiller, a silhouette against the stars.

The stars!

Mia looked up and felt her mind get blown.

*"Wow!"*

The sky was alive. Billions of tiny little twinkling points, from horizon to horizon.

"You probably won't see them like this back home," said Bear. She could hear the smile in his voice. "There's too much light pollution drowning them out. But out here, there's absolutely nothing to get in the way."

Mia made her way to the back of the boat and took the tiller from Bear.

"I can't see the compass," she realized.

"We can navigate by the stars, like our ancestors." Bear's outline pointed up. "See the Big Dipper?"

Mia recognized the constellation, like a big ladle. It was one of the things she *could* see at night back home.

accompanied by a few hundred little friends. Now, it had about a billion.

"See the edge? Those two stars? Follow them up …" Bear's finger moved upward. "And they point at that star there, the North Star. That star stays fixed while the others rotate around it, and it's always in the north – or from our point of view, about one inch to the right of the top of the mast. So as long as you keep the North Star there, we'll be on course. Got that? Awesome! See you in a couple of hours!"

Mia was left alone at the tiller again, steering *Ursula* like a starship through space.

Soon the new day dawned, and for the first time in her life Mia saw the sun come up. A ball of red fire rose up from the horizon, turning yellow as it got higher. The sky faded from dark to gray to blue, and color returned to the world. Clouds floated on the horizon ahead, like piled-up giant cotton balls sitting on a glass surface. She pointed them out when Bear came up on deck.

"Those are the first I've seen since I came on board."

Bear looked pleased.

"That's cumulus cloud, and it usually hangs over land. The temperature difference between land and sea makes water droplets form in the air."

"So, that's our island?" Mia asked.

"That's our island!" Bear agreed with

a smile. "Right on course, too. Go, us! I couldn't have done it without you, Mia."

Mia felt a proud glow inside her.

But the land was still a long way off, and *Ursula* wasn't exactly fast. They plodded on, and Bear and Mia kept up their routines. Bear had stretched out a couple of tarpaulins on deck overnight, and in the new light Mia could see that they were covered with dew – thousands of tiny droplets of water. Bear ran this into a bottle for drinking later. They had a breakfast of dried fish strips, and a bowl of canned fruit from the cabin. They took turns on the tiller. They checked the solar still for water. They pumped.

The cumulus cloud slowly got closer. After a few hours, Mia could see something dark on the horizon below

it. At first it was just a dark line, but gradually it grew and spread out. Then she began to see colors. Greens and browns.

Bear studied the island through the binoculars.

"Trees and plants," he said approvingly. "That's good. It means there'll be fresh water too."

Once Bear was back on the tiller, Mia took the binoculars so that she could see the island for herself. It was surrounded by cliffs, with waves smashing hard against them.

"Um, Bear," she said. "Where are we going to land?"

"Good question. We'll go around and see what we find."

And so, they had to wait even longer as *Ursula* crept around the island's coast. Mia watched it pass by, inch by inch. Even if she and Bear just stayed on the island until rescue came, she hoped that they would be able to patch *Ursula* up properly. Mia had grown fond of the old boat and she deserved good treatment. *Ursula* had her ways – very particular ways. But as long as you remembered that the boat was the boss, not you, you could handle her. Mia felt pretty good that she had helped Bear bring them this far.

Mia had always felt that following someone else's instructions made you less free. But she realized she had been wrong. In fact, following sensible instructions just stopped you from wasting everyone's time. And in a worst-case scenario, as Mia now knew, it could save your life.

Then Mia saw it. The cliffs dropped down and she made out a flash of yellow at sea level.

"There's a sandy beach!"

"I see it!" Bear turned the front end toward the shore. "I'm going to run us aground deliberately. The bottom's sandy so we'll be fine. You'd better get back into your swimming gear. Tie a rope to the anchor, then after we hit, swim to shore with it so you can drag the anchor after you. Then we'll be good and secure."

Mia went down below to get changed.

Soon after, *Ursula* ran into the sandy bottom with a gentle bump. Immediately Mia jumped into the sea with the rope. She swam to the beach through soft, warm water and waded ashore.

Bear had dropped the sails while she was swimming. Now he heaved the anchor over the side.

"Pull it in!" he called. Mia started to pull, hand over hand. The anchor emerged from the surf. Mia tugged it with both hands up the beach to the nearest tree. She looped it around the trunk, and caught the anchor prongs on its own rope. *There, that should hold.*

Mia trotted back to the sea, quickly, because the sun-warmed sand was starting to burn her bare feet. She dived into the first wave. The bubbles rushed against her skin, and the roaring whoosh filled her ears. And

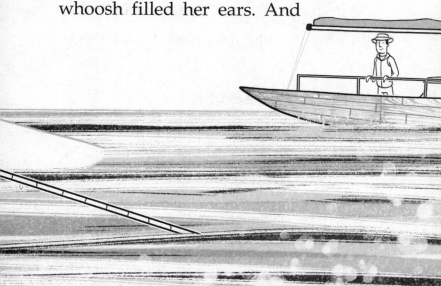

that was weird – she thought she could hear voices.

Mia broke the surface and started to swim back to *Ursula* and Bear.

*Bonk.*

An inflated ball bounced off her head. Mia stopped swimming and trod water. Huh?

Her ears were full of happy shouts and yells. Kids splashed around her in inner tubes. A whistle blew and the umpire called out.

"All players back into their tubes before we start again – that includes you, Mia!"

Mia stared in astonishment.

She was back in the pool at camp.

# 10

# END GAME

"Mia!" the umpire called again. "You need to get into your tube."

Mia's head still whirled. She was confused. What had happened to the island, to Bear, and the boat? How had she ended up back in the pool?

But there was no time for that. What seemed more important was that she was back in the middle of the game of tube polo, and she had to get on with it.

Maybe that bump on the head from the ball had knocked some weird daydream into her. Mia had heard that dreams only last a couple of seconds, even if you remember them taking much longer.

Mia remembered the reason she had ended up in the water in the first place. Her tube had sprung a leak and was half submerged next to her.

"It's gone down," she called.

"Ah, right. Time-out while I get you a new one."

The umpire went over to the pile of unused tubes by the side.

"And, Mia?" Mia's friend Suki gave her arm a gentle poke. "It might help if you follow the rules?"

Suki was being friendly, and smiling, so it didn't sound like she was being told off. But Mia still remembered that her team, the Yellows, had just lost a point because of her ignoring the right way to play, and doing her own thing.

She thought of Bear, and *Ursula*. They had only kept afloat, and reached the island, by working together and doing it right.

So, Mia just said, "No problem."

The game started again, with much splashing as the ball was chucked around the pool. A few minutes later, Mia and her new tube were right at the end of the pool. The ball smacked into her hands. The goal was next to her, and it was undefended. But from this angle, she couldn't actually get the ball into it.

It was so tempting! All Mia had to do was give the edge of the pool a hefty kick with both feet. She would go shooting backward, and then she would be able to get at the goal.

But that would mean the ball was moving, in her possession. It would be the same as carrying.

All this went through Mia's head in about half a second. The game was still going on, and the only Yellow in range was Suki. So Mia chucked the ball over to her first, and *then* she gave the end a kick. Her tube zipped away from the edge. Now Mia was in range of the goal, but with no ball.

Meanwhile Suki had caught the ball, but she didn't have anyone clear to pass it to. Except Mia, who now had a clear shot at an empty goal.

"Take it!" Suki shouted, at the same

time that she passed the ball back. Mia
grabbed it and threw it into the goal, all
in one movement. The umpire blew her
whistle and the Yellows had tied!

It felt good to score the goal, but it felt

even better when Mia thought how she had done it. By working with the rest of her team.

The next goal came very quickly, and it was the Yellows again. This time Mia was at the other end of the pool and she didn't have much to do with it. She was happy that her teammates got their own chance. Then the last whistle went, and the Yellows had won.

After the game, Mia got changed and trotted down the track to the tents. There was just time to hang her gear and towel up to dry, then get to the next activity. She found herself alongside Sophie, who was in the next tent.

"Oh, yeah, I thought about doing tube polo," Sophie said when she learned what Mia had been doing. "I'm okay with swimming, but not floating. I feel seasick right away."

Mia smiled. "I know a great way to fight seasickness," she said. She held up her wrist to demonstrate. "You press on your wrist, and ..."

Her voice trailed off in amazement.

There was something on her wrist. A strip of cloth.

It was the motion sickness bracelet that Bear had made for her. She could feel the wad inside it.

"Yes?" Sophie asked politely. Mia remembered what she had been saying.

"Oh. Um. Yes. You press on your wrist, and that stimulates the nerves and stops your brain from getting confused, so you don't feel sick."

"Okay. Maybe I'll give it a try." Sophie looked doubtful, but she went off to her tent, and left Mia staring at her wrist again. She was still wearing that bracelet! How was that possible?

There was only one way it *could* be possible.

The whole sailing challenge with Bear really had happened.

Mia's mind was still whirling as she slowly made her way back to the next activity, with her hands in her pockets. She felt herself touch the compass –

the one Joe had given her. When she checked it, it just had the normal four directions. She looked but couldn't see a fifth point anywhere.

How could her memories of her adventure with Bear be so real?

Two impossible things had both happened in a very short time.

*Hmm*, Mia wondered. *Were the two things connected?* Had the compass somehow taken her to Bear?

She walked on more thoughtfully. Then she became aware of raised voices. Two boys were arguing.

"Oh, honestly, you're always doing that!"

Mia couldn't see what the problem

was, but one of them stormed away. The other boy was left alone, looking unhappy. Whatever their issue was, it sounded like something that the boy was doing was making him and his friends unhappy.

Like Mia used to do.

Mia looked at the bracelet again. And then at the compass.

Could it do its thing again, for someone who really needed it?

There was only one way to find out.

The boy was moping off. Mia hurried over to catch up.

"Hi!" She realized she didn't know his name. "Um – how's it going?"

"It's terrible," the boy grumbled. "Camp's terrible. I'm terrible Everything's terrible."

"Well, you know ..." Mia couldn't really think of anything helpful to say. "Here. Maybe you'd like this?"

She held the compass out. The boy gazed suspiciously at it.

"Why?" he asked.

"Just try it," Mia said confidently. "It's for you. Just consider it a gift."

## The End

Bear Grylls got the taste for adventure at a young age from his father, a former Royal Marine. After school, Bear joined the Reserve SAS, then went on to become one of the youngest people ever to climb Mount Everest, just two years after breaking his back in three places during a parachute jump.

Among other adventures he has led expeditions to the Arctic and the Antarctic, crossed oceans and set world records in skydiving and paragliding.

Bear is also a bestselling author and the host of television programs such as *Survival School* and *The Island*.

He has shared his survival skills with people all over the world, and has taken many famous movie stars and sports stars on adventures – even President Barack Obama!

Bear Grylls is Chief Scout to the UK Scouting Association, encouraging young people to have great adventures, follow their dreams and to look after their friends. Bear is also honorary Colonel to the Royal Marine Commandos.

When Bear's not traveling the world, he lives with his wife and three sons on a barge in London, or on an island off the coast of Wales.

Find out more at **www.beargrylls.com**

# THE BEAR GRYLLS

The Blizzard Challenge

The Desert Challenge

The Jungle Challenge

The Volcano Challenge

The Safari Challenge

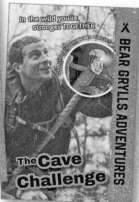

The Cave Challenge

# ADVENTURES SERIES